My Nights at the Improv

Jan Siebold

Albert Whitman & Company
Morton Grove, Illinois

Also by Jan Siebold:
Rope Burn
Doing Time Online

Library of Congress Cataloging-in-Publication Data

Siebold, Jan.
My nights at the Improv / by Jan Siebold.
p. cm.
Summary: An eighth-grader is afraid of taking risks at her new
school, but as she secretly observes an improvisational theater class
week after week, she begins to apply its principles to her own life.
ISBN 0-8075-5630-0 (hardcover)
[1. Moving, Household—Fiction. 2. First day of school—Fiction.
3. Plays—Improvisation—Fiction. 4. Acting—Technique—Fiction.
5. High schools—Fiction. 6. Schools—Fiction.
7. Mothers and daughters—Fiction.] I. Title.
PZ7.S5665Myan 2005   [Fic]—dc22   2005004590

Cover by Julie Collins.
The typeface is Janson.
The design is by Susan B. Cohn.

For more information about Albert Whitman & Company,
visit our web site at www.albertwhitman.com

To Amy, Kevin, and Nicholas

Contents

Introduction

A man named Ben once told me that in order to succeed you have to open yourself up to the risk of failure. Then, risk was a factor which hadn't entered into my boring, predictable life.

I was afraid to go out on a limb. You could fall and hurt yourself, or even die. There's safety in hugging the trunk of the tree. Unfortunately, you can't gather many nuts there, and the view isn't nearly as spectacular.

I learned a lot from Ben, even though I never met him face to face. A person can speak to you without ever talking to you. In fact, some of the most important and useful lessons I've learned lately were taught to me by a motley band of five strangers.

Thanks to them I've left my perch and ventured out onto that limb. And you know what? The view is spectacular.

1: The Projection Booth

I'm sitting in the projection booth, which looks out over the darkened school auditorium. My mother is in a classroom across the hall. She's teaching her Thursday night Community Education class in cake decorating. She can make a frosting rose that looks as if it was just picked from the garden.

I come with my mother every Thursday night. She needs someone to help her carry all of her supplies. The first night of class, Mom asked Shirley, the custodian, if there was a nice quiet place nearby where I could sit and do my homework.

"Most of the rooms upstairs here are being used for classes," Shirley told us.

Then she thought for a minute, and led us to a door across the hall from my mother's classroom. Shirley unlocked the door and turned on the light to reveal a small closetlike room.

"This was the projection booth back when we used to show reel-to-reel movies to the students. It looks out over the auditorium," Shirley explained, nodding toward the sliding-glass windows. "About the only time it's used now is during plays or concerts when a spotlight is needed."

Shirley pointed to a large spotlight on wheels which stood in the corner.

"There's a nice little desk here with its own light," said Shirley, switching on a small gooseneck lamp. "That's in case the person running the spotlight has to read a script or make notes. The door locks from the outside, but you can open it from the inside. All I'd need to do is find you a chair."

"Perfect," declared Mom.

And so I've come to think of this space as my own secret spot. I like knowing that there is a place in this school where not many other students have ever been. I stare at my reflection in the window. Some days I think my short dark hair and elfin face suit me. This isn't one of those days.

I turn off the overhead light and use only the desk lamp. That way I can see out over the dark auditorium. The stage curtains are usually open, and the area is dimly lit by several "Exit" signs.

I've discovered that it's warmer in the booth if I

crack open the sliding-glass window that overlooks the auditorium. I do so, and then get settled at the desk. Now that I'm in eighth grade, I have a ton of homework every night. I take out my English assignment, but I can't seem to concentrate on it. Just thinking about English class today makes my face go red all over again.

2: Thirty-Second Delay

Sometimes I think my brain is on a thirty-second-delay switch. In any new situation I can think of the most clever and brilliant comment to make. Unfortunately, it happens about thirty seconds after the right moment has passed.

Let me pick an example from one of thousands. In English class today we were discussing poetry. Mr. Tate, my favorite teacher, was explaining the use of alliteration.

"A poet often uses several words together that have the same beginning sounds," he said. "This tool is called 'alliteration.' It can give the poem more of a musiclike quality. Listen. *Tried and True. Hearth and Home. Death's Doorstep.* Now look at the poem on page ninety-seven. Can anyone give me an example of alliteration there?"

No one raised a hand. Mr. Tate looked around. I froze as his gaze fell on me.

"Lizzie? Can you find one?" he asked.

Here is where the thirty-second delay kicked in. I scanned the poem several times, feeling the flush that was creeping upward from my neck. After what seemed like an eternity, I mumbled, "Uh, I'm not sure."

Vanessa, the girl who sits behind me, quietly hissed. I heard a few snickers. Let me explain the hiss. You see, on my first day of school I had carried my hot pink snakeskin purse. It was fake snakeskin, of course. Who ever heard of a hot pink snake? My old friends from back home each had one, only in different colors. We had bought them together during a shopping excursion last year. Jenny's was neon green and Maria's was bright orange.

The first day of English class in my new school, Vanessa noticed it right away. I saw her make a face at another girl and point to my purse. Then she hissed like a snake.

I've since learned that being the new kid in school means being constantly sliced into thin layers and put under a microscope. Everything you do or say is closely examined and analyzed. One false move and you can be labeled an odd specimen. It's okay to be rare, but not to be odd.

Later, after the hiss, I thought of exactly the

right thing to say. I should have laughed and said, "Yeah. My pet pink boa constrictor died and I had him made into a purse." But the thirty-second delay prevented it. So I pretended not to notice and felt my face turn beet-red.

From that day on, Vanessa started hissing very quietly every time Mr. Tate calls on me. The more I let it happen, the worse it gets.

I e-mailed Jenny and Maria about it.

"Peasant!" came Jenny's reply.

Maria wrote, "Too bad we didn't buy the matching shoes. Then she'd really have something to hiss about!"

Mr. Tate had moved on to another student.

"Lee?"

A boy sitting in the front said, "The frosty frozen fields?"

"Yes. Good. The frosty frozen fields," replied Mr. Tate.

As soon as he moved on, the perfect response popped into my head. When Mr. Tate asked if I could find an example of alliteration, I should have said, *"No. Not Now. Maybe Never."* Funny, right? I think Mr. Tate would have gotten a kick out of that answer. He has a good sense of humor. More importantly, the rest of the class might have gotten a glimpse of the me that goes beyond the *stupid stammering student* that they've seen so far.

Oh, I get good grades on my written assignments. Mr. Tate must have hope for me because he keeps calling on me in class. My answers are probably a huge disappointment to him. Among my more brilliant answers have been "Uh, I'm not sure," "Er, I'm not sure," and my favorite one—"I'm really not sure." The thirty-second delay doesn't apply to just my speaking abilities. It affects my actions, too.

We were playing volleyball in gym class the other day. The score was tied with only a point left to go in the game. The other team served.

I was in the back line. After several hard-fought volleys, the ball came sailing toward me. I was convinced that the ball was heading out of bounds, so I stood there watching it. By the time I realized the ball was going to be in bounds, it was too late. I sprang into action as the ball hit the floor. I did manage to get a hefty swat at it after the bounce, though.

My teammates, including Vanessa the hisser, groaned. I got a few dirty looks, including one from the teacher.

After class I was in the locker room changing my clothes. I had just pulled off my T-shirt when

Vanessa walked by with another girl. They stopped in front of me. My book bag was sitting on the bench. Vanessa nudged it with her knee. The bag teetered and then fell to the floor. Most of my books and papers slid out.

"Oh, s-s-s-sorry," Vanessa hissed.

She and her friend giggled. I just stood there clutching my T-shirt to my chest. I felt totally exposed. Will I ever figure out how to turn off the thirty-second-delay switch?

No. Not now. Maybe never.

3: First Class

My thoughts are interrupted when some-one turns on the stage lights. I watch from above as a man walks out onto the stage from behind the curtain. The man is tall, with shaggy blond hair and a beard. Out of instinct I switch off the desk lamp so that he won't see me up in the projection booth.

He looks around and then goes offstage again. He returns with a tall stool, which he places in the center of the stage. He comes and goes, placing five more chairs in a semicircle facing the stool.

I hear voices. One by one other people arrive on stage. I almost gasp out loud when the last person comes in. It's Vanessa, the hisser from my English class! What is she doing here? I wonder. I didn't know that kids my age could sign up for Community Ed classes.

The bearded man smiles at each new person and

gestures toward the chairs. Soon all five seats are occupied. There are three men, a woman, and Vanessa.

The bearded man perches on the stool and begins to speak.

"Welcome to Improv class. I'm Ben," he announces. "I'm looking forward to getting to know all of you this semester."

The acoustics in the auditorium must be very good, because I can hear bearded Ben perfectly. He continues.

"To improvise is to make do with what you have. The idea of improvisational theater is to invent ideas on the spot. You can't rehearse Improv. If you did, it wouldn't be Improv."

The people in chairs laugh. Vanessa giggles.

Ben leans forward on his stool and says, "In order to succeed at Improv, you have to be willing to take risks. There are no wrong answers in this class. At first you'll feel like you don't have an idea in your head, but you'll find that the more exercises we do, the faster and better you'll be. The main thing is to support each other and have fun."

He pauses and then goes on.

"Even if you never get on a stage to perform improvisational theater, the skills you learn in this

class will help you be more creative and sponta-
neous in other aspects of your life."

Even though Ben can't see me, I feel like he is
speaking directly to me. It doesn't seem fair that
Vanessa is down there and I'm up here.

Ben smiles and stands up.

"Ready?" he asks.

The chair people look at each other and nod.

"Good. Then let's get started. I like to begin
each class with a warmup activity. Since we don't
know one another, let's do a little ice-breaker.
When it's your turn, I'd like you to stand up and
introduce yourself to the group. Tell us your name
and what you do."

Ben pauses and adds, "Here's the catch. You
can't talk."

The chair people look at each other and groan.

"Why don't you begin?" Ben asks, pointing to
the man in the first chair.

The man stands and faces the group. He has
dark, curly hair and a muscular build.

"Here goes nothing," he says, shrugging.

He thinks for a minute, and then points to a
ring on his finger. Then he makes motions as if
to fasten on an imaginary necklace and earrings.
He pretends to admire himself in a mirror.

He points again to the ring.

"Ring? Necklace? Jewelry?" the chair people shout. At the word *jewelry*, the man nods.

"Jewelry?" Vanessa asks.

The man makes a fluttering motion with his hand and says, "Close."

"No talking," Ben reminds him.

"Jules?" the woman guesses.

The man makes quick motions as if to say "Closer."

"Julius?" the woman asks.

The man shakes his head from side to side.

The chair people pause to think.

"Julian?" guesses Vanessa.

The man points to her and nods.

"Well done, Julian," says Ben. "Now show us what you do for a living."

Julian walks over to one of the other men and pretends to take his pulse. Then he feels the man's forehead as if checking for a fever.

"Doctor?" the pretend patient guesses.

Julian shakes his head no.

"Nurse?" the woman asks.

Julian nods. He lets out a sigh of relief and goes back to his chair.

One by one the other four people go through

the routine. There is a teacher named Mark who has short black hair and glasses. (He acts out "On your mark, get set, go!)

An accountant named Frank pretends to eat a hot dog. It takes a while for the group to get *frank-furter*. Frank looks to be the oldest member of the group. He is balding and slightly overweight.

The woman is named Mary. She acts out "Will you marry me?" Mary is a lawyer. She has dark skin and a short mannish haircut which somehow looks very feminine on her.

Finally it's Vanessa's turn. She stands and moves to the center of the group. Her auburn hair is swept up into a high ponytail. She giggles and raises her arms in front of her as though she's gripping something. She appears to be driving an imaginary vehicle.

"Car?" guesses Julian.

Vanessa shakes her head and keeps driving. She makes big motions in the shape of a rectangle.

"Truck?" asks Frank.

Vanessa makes smaller rectangular motions.

The group is quiet for a moment.

"It's a van," she announces.

The group is silent. Then Mary shouts, "Vanessa!"

"Yes!" squeals Vanessa.

"Good," says Ben. I wonder why he didn't reprimand Vanessa for talking out loud. Maybe he's going to give her special treatment because she's so young. If I were down there, I would want to be treated just like the adults.

Next Vanessa pretends to read and write. Mark guesses right away that she is a student.

Well, duh. How hard was that to figure out?

Vanessa scurries back to her chair.

Ben asks each member of the group to stand and tell the others why he or she is there.

Julian says that he has been watching a lot of Improv shows on television, and that it looks like fun. Mark explains that he'd like to be able to improvise more in his teaching.

"I practically have to rehearse my spelling tests ahead of time," he says. "I'd like to be more natural with my students."

Ben nods and says, "Good. Frank?"

Frank wipes his forehead with a handkerchief.

"I work with numbers all day," he explains. "I need to break out of my office and have a little fun. I also thought it would be a good way to meet people."

He looks anxiously from person to person.

The other members of the group nod and smile. Frank seems to relax. He sits back down.

"Mary?" Ben asks.

Mary is dressed in a dark blue business suit. I can see the flash of a gold pin on her lapel.

"As a lawyer, I need to think on my feet," she says. "A judge or jury can spot hesitation or uncertainty a mile away."

The group nods as Mary sits down.

"And Vanessa?" asks Ben.

Vanessa aims her explanation not at the group, but at Ben.

"I want to be an actress," she tells him. "I thought this would be a good way to get started."

It figures.

Ben stands.

"Good job, everyone," he says. "Now we're going to loosen up even more with an activity called "Think Links."

He goes on to explain, "When you do Improv, you have to be good at making connections between things. On the surface those things may not seem to have any relationship to each other. You have to create the relationship. I'm going to throw out the names of two different objects. When you think of a way that they are alike or related, just call it out.

Remember, there are no wrong answers. Ready?"

The group members nod.

"Okay. A chair and a dog."

"They both have legs," says Mary.

Ben nods.

"They could both be soft and furry," says Frank.

"You sit in a chair, and you tell a dog to sit?" Mark asks.

"Good," says Ben. "Any others?"

They can both be comforting, I think to myself.

Julian jumps to his feet and says, "They can both recline!"

We still haven't heard from Vanessa.

Ben waits for a few more seconds and says, "Excellent. Let's try another one. A car and a diamond ring."

The group is quiet for a moment.

"A dog could lie on a chair," Vanessa says suddenly.

The others look at her. She is obviously still on the dog/chair question.

"Good," says Ben. "Now how about a car and a diamond ring?"

"A car and a diamond ring can both be shiny," says Mary.

My mind goes racing ahead. They are both

expensive. Parts of them are round. They can both be given as gifts.

I hear a soft knock on the door.

"Lizzie?"

It's my mother. Her class must be over.

I go to the door and say, "Be right there."

As I gather up my books, I take one last look at the stage.

"A dog and a chair could both be brown," says Vanessa.

I know that Ben told us to be supportive, but I think Vanessa is going to be just as annoying here as she is in school.

Vanessa prances into English class the next day. I hear her telling a friend about her Improv class. You mean *my* Improv class, I think.

Mr. Tate is talking about Shakespeare's *Romeo and Juliet*.

"Romeo and Juliet are often referred to as 'star-crossed' lovers," says Mr. Tate. "Can anyone tell me what is meant by that phrase?"

Since Ben's class last night, I've found myself in "Think Link" mode. For example, at breakfast this morning Mom told me to hurry up and eat my toast so we could get in the car. Hmmm. How is a toaster like a car? I wondered to myself. They both have metal parts. They can both overheat. They both are electrical.

I've been making those strange connections all day long. So when Mr. Tate asks about star-crossed lovers my mind races ahead. *Stars . . . planets . . . space . . . moon . . . galaxies. . . black holes . . .*

Usually I try not to make eye contact when Mr. Tate looks like he might call on me. Today when he looks at me, I smile.

"Lizzie?" he asks.

"Well," I begin. "I think it means that even though Romeo and Juliet loved each other, it wasn't meant to be. It just wasn't in the stars for them. In fact, their stars didn't just cross, they imploded and disappeared into black holes."

Mr. Tate chuckles. One or two kids laugh. For once, no one hisses.

"Very well put," says Mr. Tate.

I can't wait for my next Improv class.

4: Mom's Recipe

My mother lives her life according to a recipe. There's no room in her life for experimenting or straying from the directions.

My grandmother (referred to from now on as GG, which stands for Grandma Grace) always says that when Mom was a little girl, her favorite books were cookbooks. It's fitting that she grew up to be a professionally trained chef.

When I look at our old photo album, I see a mother whose life was full of spice and zest. In one picture, Mom is up to her elbows in bread dough. Her face is streaked with flour and she is sticking her tongue out at the photographer, whom I assume was my father. He died when I was four years old. All I know about his death is that it happened while he was on a rafting trip with some of his buddies.

I used to ask my mom about him once in

a while. Her stories about Dad would start out strong, but after a few minutes her sentences would hang in mid-air and then drift away like puffs of smoke after a fireworks display. Mom would lose herself in her own thoughts, and I would eventually wander away. I learned early on to stop asking.

I've pieced together other crumbs of information from a variety of sources. First of all, I've figured out that Dad must have done most of the picture-taking, because he is in very few of the photos in our album. I know from those few pictures that he was tall and lean with coal black hair. His pictures always remind me of ones that I've seen of a young Abe Lincoln.

A few summers ago I went to stay at GG's house for a weekend. I asked her to tell me about Dad. She raised her eyebrows and looked at me for a minute. Then she sighed.

"I don't suppose your mother talks about him very much, does she?" GG asked.

I shook my head. GG took my face in her hands.

"I don't know why it didn't occur to me sooner that you probably need to know more about him," GG said. "As much as your mother thinks she's moved on with her life, she really hasn't. I worry about her all the time."

GG gave me a hug and said, "Pull up a chair, Lizzie. I'll tell you everything that I remember about Robert."

From GG I found out that Dad loved board games, baseball, and the Beatles. He used to call me "Lizard" instead of Lizzie. Apparently he came up with that nickname when I started to crawl on my belly, and he called me that even after I started walking. Dad was also the one who named our dog Ringo because he was always thumping his tail on the floor like a drummer. (If I have to explain further, you don't deserve to know.)

GG told me that Dad used to love giving me rides on his shoulders. He also loved the outdoors. No one ever called him "Bob." He was definitely a "Robert." GG got out a shoebox full of old photos and showed me pictures that I had never seen before. We talked about Dad a lot that weekend.

GG told me that Mom and Dad had just started fixing up our old house before he died.

"Your mother didn't feel much like going ahead with their plans for the house after your father died," GG explained. "She just painted all of the rooms beige, hung a few pictures on the walls, and called it quits."

She looked at me.

"Ever since the accident, your mother has been extra-protective of you, Lizzie. I think she was afraid of losing you, too."

"Tell me about it," I groaned.

"You started kindergarten that fall," GG continued. "Your mother was afraid to let you ride the bus, so she drove you to and from school every single day. I tried to get her to talk about things more, but she was in too much pain. We all were."

GG's eyes filled with tears.

"I'll never forget the night that we got the phone call about your father. We just couldn't believe the news. Robert was such a good swimmer. That accident never should have happened," she said, shaking her head.

I guess that's what makes an accident an accident, I thought. But why did it have to happen to my family?

5: Comfort Food

For years my mom was the head chef at the Riverview Inn. The Inn's menu consisted mostly of "comfort food," as my mother called it—chicken and biscuits, meat loaf, roast turkey with stuffing, pork chops with applesauce. While the food was tasty and well-prepared, there were no adventures in dining at this establishment.

Last year, the owners of the Inn decided to retire and move to Florida. They sold the building to a couple who planned to turn the place into a "charming Bed and Breakfast Hotel." My mother was out of a job.

GG talked to Mom.

"Why don't you open your own business?" GG suggested. "You know you've always wanted to have a gourmet bakery and coffee shop. I'll loan you the start-up money."

Mom shook her head.

"Thanks, but it's too risky," she declared. "I've got to think about Lizzie. I can't take a chance on losing my savings, let alone yours. And I need a job that offers health insurance benefits."

So Mom took a job as cafeteria manager of the Buffalo City Schools. Talk about adventures in dining.

When Mom broke the news to me, I must admit that I threw a major fit.

"What about my school?" I asked.

"I looked into that when I went for my interview," Mom replied. "Roosevelt High School has an excellent reputation."

"But what about Jenny and Maria? They're my best friends!"

"We'll only be a few hours away by car," Mom countered. "It's not like we'll never visit. They can come to stay with you some weekends, too. And I'm planning to buy a computer so you'll be able to e-mail each other all the time."

"Bribery won't work!" I yelled. "It's not the same as seeing them all the time and being in school together!"

"I know, Lizzie, but you'll make new friends," Mom said. From the look on her face, I think even she knew how lame that sounded.

"Easy for you to say," I said coldly. "You don't have any friends."

Mom drew in her breath and then slowly let it out.

"Well, then," she said in a matter-of-fact way, "I guess it will be a chance for both of us to make new friends."

I could see tears in Mom's eyes as she turned away. It wasn't my finest hour, but I needed to use every argument that I could.

I had saved what I thought was my most powerful weapon for last.

"What about GG?" I asked. "How can you leave her here by herself? She's not getting any younger, you know."

Mom turned back to look at me. Now her voice was very firm.

"Of course I'll miss GG, Lizzie, but you know very well that she will be fine. She's a whiz on that computer of hers. We can e-mail each other every day. She's so busy with her yoga and aquatic exercise classes that she's in better shape than I am. We can visit her on weekends, and I know she'll visit us. She's been spending the last few winters in Florida with Aunt Bess, anyway. And you can spend as much of next summer with her as you like."

I knew that I was defeated. To make matters worse, Ringo got sick last spring. In June we had to have him put to sleep. Mom and I were heartbroken. We were both weepy for days afterward. When we could finally talk about him without crying, Mom tried to be philosophical. She said he had had a long and happy life, and that we wouldn't want him to be in pain anymore.

"He probably died because he didn't want to move to Buffalo, either," I said coldly. Then I went to my room and cried some more.

We sold our old house and moved to Buffalo. We rented an upper flat in a house on the east side of the city. Mom didn't want to buy a home until she knew the city better.

Her new job consists of sitting at a desk most of the day. She orders food and supplies, and tries to come up with new, creative ways of using government surplus cheese. I don't think it's what she had in mind when she went to culinary school.

Our apartment is in an old Polish neighborhood. The corner bakery advertises things like paczkis and ciastos. I'm not sure what they are, but the smell coming from inside the bakery is wonderful. A market on the opposite corner offers home-made pierogis and Polish sausage.

A man named Leon Wardinski lives downstairs. His son, Leon Jr., owns the house. Leon Jr. lives around the corner with his wife and kids.

"Dad just came here from Poland," Leon Jr. explained to us. "I moved him over here after my mother died. He doesn't speak much English. He's quiet and keeps mostly to himself. You may see him outside a lot. He loves gardening, so he takes care of the yard and flower beds for me."

Mr. Wardinski and I have a ritual. Whenever our paths cross, he smiles and nods.

"Hi, Mr. Wardinski," I say.

Mr. Wardinski smiles and nods again. We stand for a painfully awkward three to five seconds, and then I say, "Well, bye."

Mr. Wardinski smiles and nods again. How do you say "Get me out of here!" in Polish? I wonder.

6: Second Class

I'm safely settled into my projection booth. It's hard to concentrate on my homework while waiting for Ben and the Improv class to appear. I looked on Mom's Community Education schedule after last week's class. Ben's class starts and ends a half-hour after Mom's class. That means I'll always miss the last part of Improv. I'll have to get as much as I can from the first half-hour each week.

Finally I see the stage lights go on. Ben comes onstage carrying a cardboard box. He puts it on the floor, and then sets up the stool and chairs as before. The others start to arrive. Vanessa waltzes in and goes to her chair. She is wearing jeans and a T-shirt, and her ponytail pokes through the back of her baseball cap. She seems to feel right at home with the group. I'm a little jealous. I'd probably feel too self-conscious to even think straight.

I notice that Mary is dressed casually like the

others tonight. She must have had time to go home and change after work, I think.

Ben begins by saying, "Tonight we're going to focus on pantomime. Pantomime is an important skill to have in improvisational theater. It's a critical way of communicating your ideas to the audience and your fellow actors. Let's begin with a simple exercise."

He pulls a paper bag out of the box.

"This bag contains slips of paper which have simple feelings or emotions written on them," Ben explains. "You're going to take turns acting them out so that the rest of the class can guess what you are feeling. They must guess the exact word on the paper."

Ben looks at the group.

"Who wants to go first?" he asks.

Mark, the teacher, stands and says, "I will."

He pulls a slip of paper out of the bag and faces the group. He wraps his arms around himself and starts to shiver.

"Cold?" Julian guesses.

Mark shakes harder and makes his teeth chatter.

"Frigid?" says Frank.

Mark shakes his head and continues to shiver.

"Freezing!" shouts Mary.

Mark nods and smiles. He sits down.

Vanessa raises her hand.

"Can I go next?" she asks.

Ben nods and holds out the bag.

Vanessa pulls out her piece of paper and reads it. She thinks for a moment, and then crosses her arms and starts to pace back and forth.

"Nervous?" asks Frank. "Anxious?"

She shakes her head and continues to pace. She stops and looks at her watch, then starts to pace again.

"Late?" Mary guesses.

Vanessa shakes her head again.

She repeats her motions, this time looking around as if she is waiting for someone.

"Worried?" asks Julian.

"Yes!" Vanessa squeals. She high-fives Julian on the way back to her chair.

"Good, Vanessa," says Ben. "That was a tough word."

It wasn't *that* tough, I think to myself.

Julian acts out "shocked" by pretending to plug in a cord and getting zapped. Mary does a great job of being "annoyed" by a pesky mosquito. The group guesses "exhausted" after Frank jogs around in a circle, then collapses to the floor, panting.

"Excellent," says Ben. "Next we're going to move on to situational pantomime, but first I want you to watch a short video of the French master of pantomime, Marcel Marceau."

Ben goes offstage and wheels in a TV and VCR on a cart. He parks the cart so that I can't see the screen. I am frustrated beyond belief. Why couldn't he show the video during the last half-hour of class? Luckily, the segment is only about five minutes long. The group was obviously impressed by it. I make a mental note to look up Marcel Marceau on the Internet or to check the public library for a video.

"Okay," says Ben. "That was pretty amazing, wasn't it?"

The members of the class nod.

Ben sits down on his stool.

"Situational pantomime is a little more involved because you have to break every action into a series of steps in order to communicate what you're doing. For example, if you were going to break down making a peanut-butter sandwich, what would some of the steps be?" he asks.

"Slicing the bread," suggests Julian. "Or taking a slice of bread out of its bag?"

"I think that unscrewing the jar of peanut butter

would come first," argues Mary. "That seems a little more concrete than trying to get across the idea of bread."

"Would you pretend to hold the knife, or would you use your finger as the knife?" asks Vanessa.

I give a little snort.

"At the end you could pretend to chew very slowly, like the peanut butter is sticking to the roof of your mouth," offers Mark.

Ben smiles and says, "Now you see what you're up against. There are no set rules for this activity, except to act out each step of your pantomime as clearly and precisely as you can."

Ben goes over to the box and pulls out a different bag. He looks from person to person.

"Who's ready to act out a situation?" he asks.

Julian shrugs and stands. "I'll give it a try," he says.

After reading his slip of paper, he rolls his eyes and shakes his head.

He pretends to scoop up something into his arms. He cradles the imaginary something like a sleeping baby. He kisses the imaginary something. Then he wrinkles his nose and sniffs. He pretends to lay his "whatever" back down and bends over it. He makes a motion like he's pulling at something with his fingertips.

He's changing a baby's diaper, I think.

"He's changing a baby's diaper!" shouts Frank.

Julian smiles and takes a bow.

"Excellent," says Ben. "Next?"

Vanessa stands. She chooses her slip of paper, then turns to the group. She begins to stomp around in a circle and shakes her fist in the air. She stops and squats as if she is examining something on the ground.

Just then I hear a knock on the door. Mom's voice calls, "Ready, Lizzie?"

I look at the stage. Vanessa is still squatting. The other members of the group look puzzled.

With a sigh, I pick up my books and open the door. Now I'll never know what Vanessa was trying to do. Of course, the rest of the class may never figure it out, either. I wonder if Mom would consider changing her class time.

7: Smiles and Nods

I was still thinking about English class on my way home from school today. Mr. Tate had been reviewing for a test. We were going over alliteration.

"Who remembers what it means?" Mr. Tate asked.

I raised my hand.

"Lizzie?"

"It's when there's a group of words that start with the same letter. Like Marcel Marceau the mime."

I heard Vanessa give a little gasp. I forced myself to stare straight ahead.

"Yes, very good," said Mr. Tate.

He continued with the review. It was all I could do to keep from laughing out loud.

When I got home, I ran into Mr. Wardinski in

the front entryway. He was checking his mailbox.

We ran through our ritual of smiles and nods. Then I went upstairs to our apartment. As soon as I opened the door, a wonderful aroma filled the hall. I remembered that Mom was going to put chicken stew in the crockpot for dinner.

Instinctively, I took a big whiff. From the bottom of the stairs, I heard Mr. Wardinski do the same thing. I turned to look down at him. He smiled and nodded. I went in and closed the door.

After dropping my backpack on my bedroom floor, I went to the kitchen. I called Mom at work to tell her I was home. She's a bit paranoid about my being at home alone. After that, I lifted the crockpot lid and stirred the savory stew. I could see big pieces of white meat mixed with slices of carrots and onions. As usual, Mom had made enough for an army. A dozen fluffy golden biscuits sat in rows on a cooling rack next to the stove.

I took another big whiff and thought of Mr. Wardinski downstairs. I wondered if he cooked much for himself. Maybe we couldn't speak the same language, but I had learned from Ben's class the night before that there are other ways to communicate.

I grabbed a bowl from the cupboard and ladled

out a big helping of chicken stew. I also put three biscuits on a plate.

Balancing the plate on top of the bowl, I went downstairs. I set the bowl and plate on a small bench that was outside Mr. Wardinski's door. I knocked.

Mr. Wardinski opened the door. He smiled and nodded.

"Would you like some chicken and biscuits?" I asked.

I pointed to the food and made motions as if I was eating. Then I pointed to Mr. Wardinski. I picked up the bowl and plate and held them out to him.

Mr. Wardinski's eyes grew wide. He nodded and smiled.

"Dziekuje," he said.

"You're welcome?" I guessed.

Mr. Wardinski took the food and set it on a small table inside the door. Then he turned back to me and paused. He gestured for me to enter. I stepped inside.

We were in the living room. I looked around. A couch and two armchairs were grouped in front of the fireplace. I could see into the dining room beyond. Both rooms looked neat and clean.

A framed photograph stood on the table next to the food that I had brought. It was a picture of Mr. Wardinski and a woman. He saw me looking at it.

"Your wife?" I asked, pointing to the photo.

"Tak," said Mr. Wardinski. "Helena."

He picked up Helena's picture and then patted his stomach. He pointed to the photo again and then to the food.

"Your wife was a good cook?" I guessed.

Mr. Wardinski smiled and nodded. Just then we heard the front door to our house open. I peeked out into the entryway. It was Mom. She looked surprised to see me.

"Is everything all right?" she asked cautiously.

"Sure," I said. "Come say hi to Mr. Wardinski. I hope it's okay if I brought him down some chicken and biscuits."

Mom stepped inside.

"Hello, Mr. Wardinski," she said.

Mr. Wardinski smiled and nodded.

"Dziekuje," he said, pointing to the food.

"That means thank you," I translated.

"You are very welcome," Mom replied. She looked at me and smiled.

"That's a picture of Mrs. Wardinski," I explained.

"Her name was Helena. She was a good cook, too."

"I'm sure she was," said Mom.

We smiled and nodded for a little while longer, and then Mom and I went upstairs.

"How did you know what Mr. Wardinski was saying about his wife?" Mom asked on the way up the stairs.

"I guess I just have a knack for languages," I replied.

Thank you, Ben. Merci, Marcel Marceau.

8: Third Class

anessa is missing from class tonight. Maybe she was spooked by what I said in English class, I think gleefully. Ben decides to start without her. He is perched on his stool facing the other four members of the group.

"Tonight we are going to focus on flexible thinking," he begins. "The idea is to think of different ways of looking at something . . . an object, a person, an idea. Let's start with an exercise called 'Pass the Object.'"

Ben goes over to the box on the floor. He pulls out a plastic ruler and holds it up.

"We're going to pass this ruler from person to person. You'll take turns pretending that it's something else. Try to think beyond the normal uses of a ruler. You can say one or two sentences to let us know more about what it is. Here's an example."

Ben holds the ruler like a baseball bat. He swings.

"Home run!" he shouts, jumping up and down.

He looks at the group.

"See what I mean?" he asks.

The group members nod. Ben hands the ruler to Mark, who stares at it and thinks for a moment. He thrusts the ruler in front of him and strikes the pose of a swordsman.

"En garde!" he yells, jabbing with the ruler.

He passes the ruler to Julian, who pretends to draw the ruler from his imaginary gun holster.

"Put your hands up," Julian orders.

Mary holds the ruler over Julian's head like a fairy wand and says, "Poof! You're a frog!"

Frank uses it like a gear shift. He makes *vroom-vroom* noises, and pretends to peel out in a racecar.

The group passes the ruler around one more time. It becomes an orchestra conductor's baton, a flute, a telescope, and a lollipop.

"Very good," says Ben.

Just then Vanessa comes in, wiping her eyes. She looks upset.

"Sorry I'm late," she says, sniffling.

The members of the group look at each other. Ben looks at Vanessa.

"Everything okay?" he asks lightly.

Vanessa nods and sits down on the empty chair.

"I had some trouble getting a ride," she answers. She takes a deep breath, then looks around and asks, "So what are we doing?"

Ben explains that we are working on flexible thinking activities.

"You'll see what I'm talking about when we do this next activity," he says.

He looks at Vanessa again.

"Sure you're okay?" he asks.

Vanessa nods.

"All right," says Ben. "Then let's get started with an activity called 'Why Is It There?' I'll name a place or a scene. Then I'll hold up an object. Your job will be to justify the existence of that object in that place. In other words, why might it be there? Ready?"

Everyone nods.

"Okay," says Ben. "The place is the United States Senate."

He reaches into the box and holds up a basketball.

"Why is it there?" he asks, pointing to Mary.

"Hmm," says Mary slowly. "Because the senators are discussing a law about how much air you can put in a basketball?"

The group laughs.

"Good," says Ben. "Frank?"

Frank thinks for a moment, then says "It's because Michael Jordan is coming to testify about the quality of the air up there."

Everyone laughs again.

"Julian?" asks Ben.

Julian chuckles and says, "I think the senators will use it to bounce ideas off each other."

The group groans.

"Great," says Ben. "Mark?"

Mark thinks, then says, "It's because the U.S. Army wants to study the use of zone defense."

"Excellent," Ben says, laughing. "Vanessa?"

Vanessa takes an extra-long time to think. I wonder how much time I have left before Mom's class ends. I wish Vanessa would hurry.

After what seems like an eternity, she shakes her head. She looks at Ben and says, "I know what I want to say, but I just can't think of a way to say it."

"Go ahead and try," suggests Ben. "Take your time."

No, I think. Hurry up.

"Well," Vanessa begins. "I was thinking of the phrase 'on the ball,' but I just can't think of how to work it in."

Ben looks from person to person.

"Any suggestions?" he asks.

"How about . . . the senators want to prove to the voters that they are on the ball?" Julian proposes.

Everyone nods.

Ben stands.

"I think it's important to talk about what just happened," he says. "Vanessa did a very brave thing. She asked for our help. That's what this class is all about. You're here because you want to learn. Sometimes the only way to learn is to ask questions. Thank you, Vanessa, for asking. And thank you, group, for being so supportive."

Okay, so I'll be more supportive, I think. I lean closer to the window. As I do, my elbow hits the gooseneck lamp on the desk. I grab for it, but it crashes to the floor.

The group members look up as I freeze. I hope with all my might that they can't see into the dark booth. Everyone is quiet.

After a few seconds Ben says, "Probably a custodian. Let's move on."

I let out a long, slow breath. I squat down and carefully inspect the lamp. Its metal shade is crooked, but the bulb isn't broken. I straighten the shade, but I don't dare turn on the lamp to see if it still works. I'll have to check it out next week before class starts.

I can hear the group laughing about something. I peek up over the window ledge. Ben is rummaging through his box as the group looks on.

Just then I hear a knock at the door.

"Lizzie?" Mom calls.

I gather my books and leave. On the way out, I think about how upset Vanessa was when she arrived. I wonder what that was all about.

Not that I care.

9: Elvis Has Left the Building

In every e-mail that I get from GG, she asks if I have made any new friends. I don't want to worry her, so I answer back that the kids in school are nice. I haven't mentioned Vanessa the hisser.

Today I may have really made a friend. I say that cautiously because the beginning stages of friendship are sometimes very delicate. There's a fine line between appearing too desperate or needy and acting like you don't care.

Oh, I know that it's best to just be yourself. But that hasn't worked too well for me so far in my new school. Until today.

There's a girl named Dee in my gym class. I found out her name early on because Miss Miller often gets us mixed up. We're both about the same size, and we both have short dark hair.

The similarities end there, though. Dee is

graceful and coordinated. I am not. Dee is quiet in class, but when she does speak she says funny, clever things. I've already explained about my thirty-second delay. Dee doesn't seem to mind if Miss Miller calls on her to demonstrate a skill. I live in fear of it.

Today Miss Miller was demonstrating the use of free weights for increasing upper body strength. After showing us a few exercises, she paired us up to work with the weights. I prayed that Vanessa would not be my partner. Instead, Miss Miller put Dee and me together.

At first we were just very polite with each other, smiling and passing the weights back and forth. Then, as Dee handed me the five-pound weight, I thought of Ben's "Pass the Object" activity last night.

Out of instinct, I took the weight and held it up to my mouth like a microphone. In my best Elvis Presley voice I said, "Thank you. Thank you very much."

Dee laughed. From that moment on, things loosened up. We started to talk about classes and teachers. I found out that "Dee" stands for Dorothea, an old Polish name. I told her about my encounter with Mr. Wardinski. It turns out that

Dee lives only a few blocks from me.

At one point during class, we heard Vanessa shriek after she dropped a ten-pound weight on the mat. We both looked over, and then Dee rolled her eyes at me. I could have hugged her for that.

After gym class, we were in the locker room. Dee and I happened to be next to each other in front of the mirror. We were fixing our hair. All of a sudden Vanessa's reflection appeared in the mirror between us. I froze.

"How sweet." Vanessa smirked. "Why, you two could practically be twins. I don't know which one of you to feel sorrier for."

I scrambled to think of something smart to say. Dee didn't seem to notice my thirty-second delay.

She just looked at Vanessa's reflection and said, "You wouldn't know the meaning of the word sweet, Vanessa. Go get yourself a life, would you?"

Vanessa made a face and walked away.

"I wish I knew what her problem is," Dee sighed, brushing her hair. "She doesn't have a decent word to say to anyone."

"I wish I knew, too," I replied.

So I'm not Vanessa's only victim, I thought. I don't know if that made me feel better or worse. I just knew that I wasn't going to waste another moment wondering about Vanessa's crying episode.

Dee and I finished up and left the locker room. As we went our separate ways, Dee waved and said, "See you tomorrow, Lizzie."

I nodded and waved back. At that moment it struck me that Dee was the first student in my new school to call me by name. For the first time in my life, I'm looking forward to gym class.

10: Fourth Class

Ben is sitting on his stool explaining tonight's first activity. I'm supposed to be working on an English essay that is due this week, but I'll just have to put in some overtime when I get home tonight. I don't want to miss a single moment of Improv class.

I tried out the lamp when I first arrived tonight. It doesn't work. I plan to ask Shirley for a new bulb the next time I see her. I'd bring one from home, but it's an odd little size.

"So far you've been doing a great job," Ben is saying, "but tonight we need to start working on speed. Up to now I've given you lots of time to think during each activity. However, you wouldn't have that luxury if you were really doing Improv. You'd have to think on your feet."

Ben stands.

"Let's do a quick warmup," he says. "I'll throw out a topic and then a letter of the alphabet.

As quickly as you can, give me a word or phrase that deals with the topic and begins with that letter. We'll go right down the line. Just say the first thing that pops into your mind. Remember, we're working on speed. Ready?"

The group members nod.

"Okay," says Ben. "The topic is food. The letter is S. Julian?"

"S-s-s-s-spaghetti!" Julian sputters.

"Sushi," says Mary without hesitation.

"Uh—salsa!" shouts Mark.

Frank stops to think.

"No stopping!" Ben reminds him.

"S-s-s-s-soy sauce!" Frank stammers.

"Squash!" Vanessa yells.

Not bad, I think, with all my supportive might.

"Good," says Ben. "The next topic is recreational activities. The letter is . . . H. Don't be afraid to have some fun. Let's start with Mary this time."

Almost immediately Mary says, "Horseback riding."

"Hang-gliding," says Mark.

"Hula dancing?" Frank suggests, wiggling his hips and waving his arms. The group laughs.

Vanessa wrings her hands as she tries to think of something.

Come on, Vanessa. How about hissing? Or harassing?

"Having fun?" she suggests.

Lame, I think. So much for being supportive.

"Okay," says Ben. "Julian?"

"Let's see," says Julian. "Um . . . hog-tying!"

Everyone laughs again. They go through a few more rounds.

"That was very good," Ben tells the group. "I think you're ready to step things up a bit."

The group groans as Ben continues.

"This next activity requires you to really listen to each other and to build on what is said before it's your turn. The activity is called 'Oh, yeah?' Here's how it works. I'm going to make a statement. You'll take turns trying to top it with a statement of your own. For example, if I said 'I'm a pretty good tennis player,' then you might counter with 'Oh, yeah? Well, I'm so good that I play tennis using a volley-ball net!' See what I mean?"

Everyone nods.

"Okay," says Ben. "Remember. Speed is key. Here's my statement: 'I play the piano.' Julian?"

"Oh, yeah?" Julian challenges. "Well, I play the piano and the . . . banjo."

"Oh, yeah?" offers Mary. "Well, I play the

piano and the banjo at the same time!"

Everyone laughs.

"Oh, yeah?" says Mark. "Well, I was invited to the White House to play the piano and the banjo for the president of the United States."

"Oh, yeah?" Frank chuckles. "Well, I played the piano and the banjo at my own funeral!"

Ben is laughing along with the group.

"Oh, yeah?" says Vanessa. "Well, I played the piano and the banjo at my own first birthday party!"

The group continues to laugh. I have to admit, that one wasn't bad, Vanessa.

Just then I hear my mother's knock at the door. I look at the stage. The group is getting ready for another round of "Oh, yeah?"

My mother's muffled voice comes through the door. "Lizzie?"

I gather up my untouched English books and leave.

11: Call a Toe Truck

On the way home, I notice that Mom seems more quiet than usual. I can tell that she is tired.

"How's work going?" I ask.

"Oh, fine," Mom replies.

She glances at me and smiles. It occurs to me that starting a new job is probably a lot like starting a new school.

"Are the people nice?" I ask.

What I really want to ask is, "Have you made any new friends?" I still feel bad about the comment I made about Mom not having any friends.

"Oh, yes," Mom answers. "Very nice. There's a woman named Bev in the accounting department who is especially friendly. I think she lives by herself. I was thinking of inviting her over for dinner someday soon."

Mom looks at me sideways and adds, "Maybe

after I get to know her a little better, that is."

It's just like me and Dee, I suddenly realize. Neither Mom nor I want to risk making any sudden moves that might scare away a new friend.

"How about you?" Mom asks. "How's school going?"

"Okay," I reply. "There's a girl in my gym class who is pretty nice. She doesn't live too far from us."

We're stopped at a red light.

"Well, feel free to invite her over sometime," Mom offers. Then she adds, "Whenever you feel ready, that is."

Mom and I look at each other. I nod. It's spooky. Mom and I have more in common than I sometimes think.

Back home, I turn on the computer to check my e-mail. There's nothing from Maria or Jenny. I guess they still have each other so they don't need me as much as I need them. I'm feeling totally sorry for myself when I see an instant message pop onto the screen. It's GG.

GG: Hi, Lizzie. How's it going?

Lizzie: Okay. How about you?

GG: Could be better. It was one of those days when everything went wrong.

Lizzie: Like what?

GG: For one thing, I woke up this morning with a lousy cold. I went out to my car and had a flat tire. I had to call a mechanic to come and fix it. Later on, I dropped a glass bowl and it broke into about a million pieces.

I think of Ben's "Oh, yeah?" activity.

Lizzie: Oh, yeah? Well, I had such a bad day that MY glass bowl broke into a million and ONE pieces!

GG is quick to catch on.

GG: Oh, really? Well, I stepped on one of the pieces and cut my toe!

Lizzie: Oh, yeah? Well, one of the broken pieces cut off my toe! I had to call a toe truck!

GG: Oh, yeah? Well, I had such a bad day that I'm going to go call my granddaughter just to hear the sound of her voice!

A few seconds later, the phone rings. I run to answer it.

12: Fifth Class

The gooseneck lamp is working again. Shirley must have replaced the bulb. I'll have to thank her when I see her again.

I don't have much homework tonight, so I'm sitting in the projection booth daydreaming while I wait for Ben's class to start. (Of course, I've been known to sit and daydream even if I have a ton of homework to do.)

Dee and I were in the locker room after gym class today. She asked me if I want to go to the mall tomorrow night for shopping and a movie.

When I asked Mom if it was okay, she tried to act as though it wasn't a big deal, but I could tell she was really happy about it. I know she's dying for me to make a friend here.

After Dee and I made our plans, Mom said casually, "As long as you're going out tomorrow night, maybe I'll ask Bev if she wants to grab a bite to eat after work."

I tried to act as though her plan wasn't a big deal, either, but I felt like doing a cartwheel. I'm dying for Mom to make a friend, too.

The people in the class begin to arrive. As soon as everyone is settled, Ben says, "It struck me during our last class that you are really starting to come together as a group. You are much more relaxed and comfortable with each other, so you're focusing on your thoughts and actions. Let's see if we can take that a step further tonight."

Ben stands.

"Okay," he says. "We'll warm up with a rhyming exercise. I'll give you a topic, and then I'll feed you a sentence about it. Each of you will come up with a response that rhymes with my line. This activity forces you to really listen to what was said by the others so you don't repeat one of their rhyming words. And remember, we're working on speed. Ready?"

Everyone nods.

"Okay," says Ben. "The topic is music. Here's my sentence. I heard a song on the radio."

Mary pauses briefly and says, "They played it three times in a row."

Mark chimes in with, "The bass notes sounded soft and low."

After a few seconds Frank says, "The song was mournful . . . full of woe."

It's Vanessa's turn. She closes her eyes for a moment to think.

Then she says, "I think the singer's name is Joe."

Vanessa looks at the others and shrugs.

Julian grins and says, snapping his fingers to the beat, "Play that music, Daddy-O!"

The group laughs.

"Excellent!" Ben exclaims. "You're all getting much faster. And you'll find that the more you practice, the more those rhyming words will roll right off the tip of your tongue. You can apply the same activity to making up songs."

Ben gives the group a few more sentences to rhyme. Then he says, "Let's move on to a different activity. In the last one, you sometimes had to use extra words as filler to make your sentences rhyme and follow the beat. Now we're going to practice using as few words as possible to get across an idea. This activity is called 'Countdown.' I'll throw out a topic, and every response you give the first time around can have only five words, the second time around four words, the third time around three words, and so on. Feel free to count on your fingers if you need to at first. And don't use meaningless filler words like *okay* or *well* to start or end your sentences. Ready?"

The class members nod.

"Okay. The topic is summer vacation. Mary? Five words."

Mary is silent for a moment and then says, "Let's go to the beach."

She turns to Mark, who answers in a staccato voice as he counts, "I'll - go - get - my - suit."

Ben interrupts.

"Try to speak in a natural voice," he suggests.

Frank is ready with his sentence. "I think it will rain," he says.

Vanessa counts on her fingers as she says, "Then let's do something else."

Julian answers, "What shall we do, friends?"

"Good. Four words this time around," Ben announces.

Mary doesn't miss a beat. "How about a movie?" she asks.

Mark says, "What's up at theaters?"

"*Gone with the Wind,*" Frank replies.

Everyone laughs.

"I never saw it," volunteers Vanessa.

"Can we get popcorn?" asks Julian.

"Three words," says Ben.

"Yes, no butter," says Mary pointing to Julian.

"Some candy, too?" asks Mark.

Frank shakes his head no and says, "None for you."

"How about me?" Vanessa giggles.

"If you're good," Julian tells her.

The whole group is laughing now.

"Two words!" Ben announces.

Mary says, "Let's go!"

Mark adds, "Right now!"

Frank answers, "I'll drive."

Vanessa says, "Can't I?"

"Not yet," Julian replies.

"Okay, one word!" says Ben.

"Go," says Mary.

"Bossy!" observes Mark.

"Children," says Frank.

"Behave," orders Vanessa.

"Chill!" Julian says.

Ben is laughing along with the group as they finish the final round of sentences. The group is having so much fun that I wish I was down there with them, Vanessa or no Vanessa. It occurs to me that she didn't annoy me much at all tonight. Maybe

I'm becoming immune to her evilness. Or maybe Dee's niceness helps cancel out Vanessa's meanness. Just then Mom raps on the door. It's time to go.

13: X Y Z

My only homework assignment tonight is to write a short character sketch for English class. Mr. Tate wants us to include details that really give the reader a glimpse into our character's personality.

I keep thinking of tonight's Improv class. The rhyming activity was fun, and I really liked the "countdown" of words. I've always loved word games and puzzles and playing around with language.

Maybe I could write my character sketch about an astronaut who talks countdown style in decreasing numbers of words. Or how about a math teacher whose sentences always have the same number of words? That might be hard to get across to the reader, though.

I remember a car game that Mom and I used to play called "The Alphabet Game." One of us would throw out a topic, and you had to think of things within that topic that started with each letter of the alphabet. X was always a challenge.

That gave me an idea. I played around with it in my mind for a while, and this is what I wrote . . .

Alexander B. Canfield
by Lizzie Marino

Even as a child, Alex loved tidiness and order. He would arrange the food on his plate in neat rows according to size. String beans were lined up neatly next to french fries, followed by a hot dog with one straight squirt of mustard running along its length. Peas were frustrating for Alex. They just wouldn't stay put.

Alex's closet was a sight to behold. His clothes were neatly hung in color groups. Below them, pairs of shoes and sneakers sat on the floor like cars in a parking garage. It's no wonder that Alex grew up to become a librarian.

Alex took pride in his library. He loved the fact that everything had its own special place. He was quick and efficient at locating items that his customers wanted. However, one day something unusual happened whenever Alex spoke. The words in his sentences started coming out in alphabetical order.

When Bobby Jones put on his bicycle helmet as he was leaving the library, Alex said, "Always Be Careful."

When Hazel Smith asked Alex to recommend a good book, he said, "Read Some Tolstoy." And when Mrs. Appleby, the library clerk, complained of heartburn, Alex told her, "Don't Eat Fats."

Alex's family and friends soon became used to his unusual way of speaking.

"How do you do it?" they would ask him. "How do you know what to say without even hesitating?"

Alex would shrug and answer, "I Just Know."

14: My Father, the Telephone Pole

It's Sunday night of the best weekend that I've had in a long time. Dee and I had a great time at the mall Friday night. She's coming over to spend the night next weekend. Mom had fun going out to dinner with her new friend Bev, too.

Yesterday morning, we drove back to our old town to visit GG and spend the night at her house. I called Jenny and Maria while I was there, and they popped over to GG's house to visit for a few hours. They really do seem to miss me as much as I miss them. We caught up on all of the news and vowed to be better at keeping in touch.

On the drive back to Buffalo this afternoon, I was thinking about the Improv class. I decided to try one of the activities with Mom. I told her that I had learned a new game in school (not a lie!), and explained the Think Link exercise to her.

"Sounds like fun," Mom said. "Go ahead and ask me one."

"Okay," I said, looking around the car and outside for ideas. "How is a . . . book like a . . . billboard?"

"Hmmm," said Mom.

She thought for a moment, and then said, "Well, they both have words written on them. And they both start with the letter B."

Mom thought for a few more seconds.

"They can both have pictures on them. And they were both created by someone."

"Very good," I told her. "Now you think of one."

"Let me see," Mom said as we passed a restaurant. "How is a cup of coffee like a . . . bicycle?"

"Well, they both have the letter C in them. In fact, they both have two C's."

I thought some more.

"You have to grip both of them," I went on. "And you could take a spill with each of them, too."

"That's a good one," Mom said. "I like this game. Give me another one."

I looked out the window.

"Okay," I said. "How is a telephone pole—"

Just then a Beatles song came on the radio.

I always think of Dad when I hear the Beatles.

"How is a telephone pole . . . like Dad?" I asked.

Mom stared straight ahead. She didn't say anything for a few minutes. I've crossed the line, I thought.

Then Mom cleared her throat and said, "Well, let's see. How is a telephone pole like your father? Well, they're both tall and slim. And they're both strong."

Mom and I were both quiet while she thought some more. Then she chuckled.

"I guess you could say that they're both hard-headed."

"What do you mean?" I asked.

Mom glanced at me.

"I mean that your father could be very stubborn," Mom explained. "When he made his mind up to do something, there was no stopping him."

We weren't playing the Think Link game anymore, but now that Mom had opened the door I wasn't about to close it.

Mom glanced at me. She seemed more serious now.

"Lizzie," she began. Then she stopped.

"What?" I asked. Please don't stop now, I thought.

"It's just that . . . "

Mom glanced at me again. I don't know if she realized it, but she was driving much slower. She took a deep breath, and said, "It's hard for me to talk about this."

"Well, it's hard for me not to!" I cried.

A car sped past us. The driver honked his horn and gave Mom a dirty look.

"Fair enough," she agreed. "Look. I think I'm going to pull over so we can talk. The last thing we need to do is have a car accident."

She pulled into the parking lot of a home improvement store.

"Lizzie," Mom began slowly. "I'm going to tell you something that I've never told anyone before about the weekend that your father died."

I stared at Mom and nodded.

Mom took another deep breath.

"Okay, here goes," she said, turning toward me. "Let me first say that your dad was a wonderful man. I loved him very much, and we had a very good marriage."

I nodded again. Part of me wanted to hear what Mom was going to say, but the other part of me was afraid.

"Before he left to go rafting with his buddies,"

Mom continued, "we had a terrible argument."

Mom's eyes welled up with tears.

"I wanted Robert to stay home and work on the house, but his friend Joe was pressuring him to go. You see, one of their friends was moving to California, and the rafting trip was going to be sort of a farewell for him. Robert was really torn about going."

Mom swallowed hard, and then went on.

"We quarreled right up until the time Robert left. I didn't even say good-bye to him."

By now Mom and I were both crying.

"I didn't even say good-bye," Mom whispered again, hugging me.

After a few minutes, Mom fished around in the glove compartment for some tissues. We both wiped our eyes. We sat there for a few minutes, lost in our own thoughts.

I turned to Mom suddenly.

"All couples argue from time to time," I told her. "Don't they? That doesn't mean they don't love each other."

Mom took my hand and squeezed it.

"Yes, and it's taken me years to figure that out. I know that he loved both of us very much. And he knew that we loved him. At the funeral, Joe told me that all Robert talked about on the rafting trip was you and me and our plans for the house."

Mom brushed a piece of hair out of my eyes.

"I owe you a big apology, Lizzie," she said, her eyes filling with tears again.

"For what?" I asked.

"For not talking about your dad. For keeping him from you. For letting my guilt and sorrow get in the way. For a zillion other things, too, probably."

Mom sat back in her seat and closed her eyes.

"For the longest time, I couldn't even bear to talk about Robert or say his name. GG would try to get me to talk about him, but I just couldn't," Mom explained.

"I know," I replied solemnly.

Mom looked at me and nodded.

"GG has told me some things about him," I said.

Mom laughed.

"What would we do without GG?" she asked, shaking her head. Then she looked me square in the eyes and said, "Lizzie, I thought this move to Buffalo could be a fresh start for me. Maybe I was being selfish. Are you completely miserable there? Tell me."

I thought of the Improv class, and Dee, and

Mr. Wardinski, and Mr. Tate.

"Not really," I replied. "I'm getting used to the place."

The funny thing is, I was telling the truth.

Mom looked at her watch.

"Well, we'd better hit the road again," she said. "But first promise me something?"

I nodded.

"Promise me you won't be afraid to bring up the subject of your father?"

"Okay," I said. "But you've got to promise that you'll bring up the subject once in a while, too."

"It's a deal," Mom promised.

15: First Snow

It's the next night, and I'm sitting in my bedroom doing my homework. I'm wearing a sweatshirt and sweatpants over my pajamas. I'm finally starting to warm up. I can hear Mom on the phone. I think she's telling GG about tonight's ordeal. Here's what happened.

It started snowing around noon today (and hasn't stopped). I've always loved the first snowfall of the year. It adds sparkle and life to the drab gray world of late autumn. (Although after tonight's little adventure, I don't know if I'll ever feel that way again.)

The snow made everyone restless in school. Even the teachers were buzzing about the possibility of classes being canceled tomorrow.

I hadn't worn boots or mittens to school, and my hands and feet were frozen by the time I trudged home from the corner bus stop. The wind had picked up, and the snow on our side-walk was almost knee-deep. I was surprised that Mr. Wardinski hadn't shoveled the walk, and then I remembered that he always goes to his son's house for dinner on Monday.

I hurried upstairs and let myself into our apart-ment. The automatic thermostat is set for the heat to come on before I get home every day, so the place was already cozy and warm.

I changed into a pair of drawstring pajama pants and a T-shirt, and went to the kitchen to call Mom at work.

"How's the weather there?" she asked.

"It's snowing really hard," I reported.

"I'm leaving in a few minutes, but I may be late getting home," Mom said. "From what people are saying, some of the streets haven't been plowed yet. Maybe you should go downstairs and stay with Mr. Wardinski until I get home."

"He's not home," I said. "He's probably over at Leon Jr.'s house."

"Hmm," Mom replied. "Well, you could go next door to Mrs. Drabek's house. I don't like the idea of you being there alone during this storm."

"I'll be fine," I insisted.

Mom hesitated.

"Really, I will," I told her, a note of impatience creeping into my voice.

"Well . . . okay," Mom said. "But call my cell phone right away if the power goes out or anything. We'll fix some soup and sandwiches when I get there."

"Sounds good," I replied. "See you when you get here."

When would Mom stop treating me like a baby? I wondered.

I had been in such a hurry to get inside that I hadn't picked up the mail from the entryway. I opened the door to the hall and headed downstairs in my stocking feet.

The hallway isn't heated, so it was cold and drafty. I shivered as I hurried down the steps, trying to avoid the puddles that my snow-covered shoes had made a little while earlier.

Down in the entryway, I scooped up the mail. Just as I was heading back up, I heard the door to our apartment slam shut.

I raced back up the stairs, already knowing what I would find. Sure enough, the door to our apartment was locked. I tried twisting the knob again and again. I finally gave up.

It might be a long time before Mom got home. Mr. Wardinski would probably stay at Leon's for a while, if not the whole night. I was already shivering. How long does it take someone to freeze to death? I wondered.

Maybe Mr. Wardinski had a coat in the hall closet downstairs, I thought. I headed back down and opened the closet door. Three empty coat hangers dangled from the rod. A broom and a dustpan leaned against one wall. A pair of men's rubber boots sat in the middle of the closet floor.

At least the closet might be warmer, I thought. I stepped inside and closed the door. It definitely wasn't warmer, and I didn't like standing there in the dark. I opened the door again.

We learned in science class that hot air rises, I remembered, so I climbed the stairs again and sat down on the top step. It didn't seem any warmer up there, either. I guess in order for hot air to rise, there has to be some hot air in the first place. I breathed into my hands to warm them up a little. Being at Mrs. Drabek's house didn't seem like such a bad idea after all.

To pass some time, I looked through our mail. There was a sheet of coupons from a pizzeria, a letter from an insurance company, and what was probably an electric bill. I was disgusted that I had locked myself out of the house because of those few pieces of boring mail.

I was really starting to shake from the cold. I thought of Improv class when Mark had acted out the word "freezing."

"I need to improvise my way out of here," I muttered.

I remembered the flexible thinking activity where the group had to find a new use for different objects.

"Why not?" I said out loud.

I stood up and looked around. There had to be something there that would help me.

Mom had hung our old kitchen curtains on the window at the top of the hallway stairs. They were made of some kind of lightweight flowered cloth, but there was enough fabric that I could wrap them around me several times—if I could get them down, that is.

The curtain rod was way above my reach. The windowsill was too narrow for me to stand on, and it didn't seem like a good idea to try such a stunt at the top of a flight of stairs.

I looked up at the curtains. The rod appeared to be clamped at each end into a metal bracket. It looked easy enough to lift the rod out of the brackets, if I could find something to push it.

I went downstairs and opened the closet door. Grabbing the broom, I hurried back up to the window.

Placing the end of the broom handle against the curtain rod, I pushed as hard as I could. The broom handle slipped and banged against the windowpane. The last thing I need to do is break the glass, I thought.

I turned the broom around to the other end and pushed against the rod. The broom's bristles held the rod in place, so I pushed harder. The rod was clamped in more tightly than I had thought, so I pushed with all my might. The curtain rod popped out of the left bracket, and the bristles of the broom kept it from falling. I carefully lowered the broom along with one end of the curtain rod. Grasping the rod, I twisted and pushed at the same time. The other end popped out of its bracket.

I lowered the rod and slipped the cloth loops of the curtains off easily. I stood the rod in the corner.

Before wrapping myself in the fabric, I returned the broom to the closet below and brought up Mr. Wardinski's rubber boots. I didn't think he'd mind if I borrowed them.

I sat on the top step and put on the boots. They had no lining and they were much too big for me, but at least they would provide another layer. I wrapped one curtain panel around my legs, and the other around my upper body. Not bad, I thought.

The wind rattled the door at the bottom of the stairs. I could hear snow brushing against the glass of the window above me. I hoped that Mom wasn't stuck in the snow somewhere. I leaned against the wall and settled in for the wait.

I thought about our car ride home from GG's yesterday. I wondered if Mom was still okay with our whole conversation about Dad. She hadn't said anything about it at breakfast, but she had seemed pretty cheerful this morning.

Maybe I should test Mom by throwing out Dad's name tonight, just to see how she would react. Or should I wait a day or two and let the dust from our talk settle a bit? I wondered.

I sat there puzzling over the question for a long time. I was still cold, but at least I had stopped shaking.

Finally I heard the door open downstairs. It was Mom. She let herself in, stamping the snow off her shoes.

"Hi," I said from the top of the stairs.

Mom looked up, startled.

"Lizzie!" she cried.

"I locked myself out," I said, sheepishly.

Mom looked upset. She started to say something, but I cut her off.

"And please don't say 'I told you so,'" I said as I stood up.

She stared at me for a few seconds. Then she nodded.

"I don't know if I would have thought of using the curtains," she said, climbing the stairs.

Mom unlocked the door.

"Let's get inside where it's warm," she said, putting her arm around me.

Later, while we were eating our soup and sandwiches, we laughed about my outfit. Mom said that she was impressed by my resourcefulness.

She tilted her head and looked at me.

"You're getting more and more like your father every day," Mom said. "He was very good at making the best of a bad situation."

I grinned. I wouldn't have to test Mom after all.

16: Sixth Class

I'm sitting in the booth waiting for Improv class to begin. Vanessa is missing again tonight, and so is Mary. Just as Ben is about to get started without them, someone knocks at the projection booth door.

"Lizzie?"

It's Mom. I open the door.

"Hi, honey," Mom says. "I must have left my box of flower tips on the back seat of the car. Would you run down and get it for me?"

I glance behind me toward the window of the booth. I know that class is about to begin. I look at Mom.

"Sure," I say.

Mom hands me the car keys. I grab my backpack and place it in the doorway of the booth so that I don't get locked out. Mom goes back to her classroom.

I take the stairs two at a time and hurry out to the parking lot. It's just starting to get dark. We're parked in a space close to the school building. I unlock the car and open the back door. I look in the back seat, but I don't see the box of tips. Maybe it slid off onto the floor, I think to myself.

I lean down to get a better look. I can see the box sticking out from under the front seat on the other side of the car. I can't reach it from here, so I close the door and walk around to the other side.

Just then a beat-up old car pulls in next to where I was just standing. I glance over and see Vanessa sitting in the front seat. I can't see who is driving. I squat down quickly next to our car so that she doesn't see me.

I hear Vanessa's door open.

"You better be out here when I come to pick you up," a woman's voice snarls from inside the car.

"Don't worry, I will," Vanessa answers back.

"Well, you didn't mind keeping me waiting last week," the woman retorted. "If that happens tonight, you'll walk home."

"I said I'll be here," Vanessa snaps.

I hear Vanessa's shoes on the gravel. I remain frozen in my squatting position. I hardly dare to breathe.

"And one more thing, Miss High-and-Mighty," the woman calls sharply. "Those dirty dishes will be waiting for you when you get home tonight. Don't think you're getting out of doing them just because of this class. I should never have agreed to let you sign up for it. It has been nothing but a royal pain for me to run you back and forth to school every Thursday night."

"Yeah, imagine me wanting to learn something new," shouts Vanessa, slamming the car door.

I hear her stomp off toward the school. A few seconds later, the car backs around and speeds off.

It stands to reason, I think, that snarling mothers breed hissing daughters.

I stay in my position for a few more minutes. I'm just about to stand up when a car pulls in right next to me. Leaping to my feet, I open the door of our car and pretend to look inside. I hear a car door open behind me.

"Lose something?" asks a familiar voice.

I turn around and face Mary from Improv class. She gets out of her car and looks at me. She is smaller in person than she looks on stage.

I stare at Mary blankly for a few seconds. To her, I am a perfect stranger, but I feel as if I know her.

What if she knew that I had been spying on her all these weeks?

"Can I help you find something?" she asks. "I saw you squatting on the ground, and I thought maybe you lost something."

My turn to improvise, I think.

I hold up Mom's car keys and smile.

"Just dropped these," I say. "My mother is teaching a class, and she sent me out to the car to get something."

Mary nods.

"Thanks, though," I add.

"No problem," says Mary. "Bye."

I watch as Mary hurries toward the school. I lean against our car for a few minutes, then I grab the box of flower tips and head back inside where my calm, friendly mother is teaching her class.

After delivering the frosting tips to my mother, I settle back into the booth. I must have missed the warmup exercise, because Ben is congratulating the group on a job well done.

"Let's move on to another flexibility activity," he says. "It's called 'Interview the Experts.' One of you will pretend to be a TV news reporter interviewing a panel of four experts. I'll tell them about their area of expertise in a minute. Every time I call out a word, the news reporter must use that word in the next question. Understand?"

The group members nod.

"You have to be ready to switch gears in a hurry," Ben tells the group. "The idea is to react quickly to the new information that is thrown at you."

Ben pauses.

"On the first night of class we talked about risk-taking," he says. "Now that you're getting comfortable with Improv and with each other, it's time for you to break out of your shells a little more. Dare to go where you haven't gone before."

The members of the group look at each other and nod.

"Okay," says Ben. "Who wants to go first as news reporter?"

Vanessa shrugs and raises her hand.

"Great," Ben says. "You come over here and face the group, Vanessa. Here's your microphone."

He hands Vanessa a ruler. She takes it and holds it up to her mouth. Ben turns toward the rest of the group.

"The rest of you are experts on the subject of fashion," he announces.

Everyone laughs.

"Take it away, Vanessa," Ben says. "We'll start with an easy word. Your first sentence must contain the word *boots*."

Vanessa clears her throat.

"So tell me," she begins in a mock-serious tone. "Is it true that boots will be big in the fashion world this fall?"

Mary speaks up first.

"Oh, yes," she gushes. "High boots, low boots, in-between boots—they're all hot right now."

"Absolutely," Julian adds. "Why, get yourself a pair of rubber hip boots and you'll make a splash at any event."

Everyone groans. Ben chuckles.

Mark hesitates, and then says, "Wear them as a pair, or mix and match them for a sensational look."

Frank follows up by saying, "And just wait until you see the new line of beachwear boots."

"Good," Ben calls. "The next word is *chicken*."

Vanessa giggles and rolls her eyes. She thinks for a few seconds.

"And what about other accessories?" she asks. "I hear that chicken feathers are all the rage this season."

Mark jumps right in.

"Oh, yes," he says. "There'll be a whole lot of plucking going on this fall."

"And a whole lot of clucking going on," adds Frank.

Everyone laughs.

"Chicken feathers are inexpensive, yet very chic," says Mary. "Or should I say chick?"

"Yes," agrees Julian. "You can pick up a darling little chicken-feather handbag for just a few bawk-bawk-bucks."

Again, everyone laughs. Grinning, Ben says to Vanessa, "Your last word is *pizza*."

Pausing for just a moment, Vanessa asks, "And what will the well-dressed teenager be wearing this fall for a casual evening of pizza and a movie?"

"If he's a slob like me, he'll be wearing the pizza," exclaims Julian.

"That's why the color red is so important this fall," adds Mary.

Frank chimes in. "And the newest fragrance for young men is Eau de Pepperoni," he says.

"That reminds me, isn't it time for lunch?" asks Mark.

The whole group laughs.

"Excellent!" Ben proclaims.

The class members take turns being the news

reporter. Julian interviews a panel of experts on global warming. Mary's group answers questions about food. There is a lot of laughter. Mark is just about to take his turn when Mom knocks at the door.

I pick up my book bag and reluctantly go to the door.

17: Point of View

I f you would have told me a few weeks ago how today was going to turn out, I never would have believed it.

For one thing, Mom and I invited Mr. Wardinski to come up for dinner tonight. He arrived exactly on time, with a bouquet of flowers. He wore a button-down shirt and a tie, and seemed very excited to come.

Mom made roast beef, mashed potatoes, and green beans Caesar. She also made a seven-layer chocolate cake for dessert. We still smile and nod a lot when we're with Mr. Wardinski, but the awkwardness is gone. He is picking up more and more English, and we're learning some Polish words, too. We had a great time. I never would have predicted that happening.

The biggest surprise came in English class today. We had read a short story about a woman who uses her only child in a plot to seek revenge against an old enemy. The plot backfires, and she loses everything, including her beloved child. The story was pretty depressing.

Mr. Tate was talking about "point of view."

"The mother in this story comes across as selfish and cruel," he said.

Some students nodded in agreement.

"But she must have had strong reasons for doing what she did," Mr. Tate continued. "The author doesn't come right out and tell us those reasons, but he gives us clues about her childhood, her marriage, and some tragedies in her own life that contributed to what she did."

Mr. Tate looked at the clock.

"We have twenty minutes left," he said. "I want you to break up into pairs and come up with a statement that the mother might give in defense of her actions."

I immediately froze.

Please, please, please don't make me work with Vanessa, I prayed silently, as Mr. Tate scanned the rows.

"Let's see," he said. "The first, third, and fifth students in each row will turn around and work with the person behind them. Lee, you move over and work with Joe. Take the rest of the period to come up with your statements. You'll present them in class tomorrow."

My worst fear was realized. I was the third student in my row, which meant that I had to turn around and work with Vanessa.

My hands were shaking as I picked up my notebook and pen. I closed my eyes, took a deep breath, and turned around to face her. This is going to be the longest twenty minutes of my life, I thought.

Vanessa was sitting back in her chair with her arms crossed. She scowled when I turned around. I hugged my notebook tightly to my chest. We looked at each other for a few seconds.

Vanessa suddenly leaned forward and put her elbows on her desk. Startled, I jumped back in my chair a little.

"Let's get this over with," she snapped. "Any ideas?"

I pictured Vanessa in the role of the TV news reporter during last night's Improv class. That gave me an idea.

"Well," I said slowly. I hesitated for a moment.

"Yeah?" Vanessa asked.

"Well, instead of just writing a statement, what if we pretended that a news reporter was interviewing the mother. During our presentation one of us could be the mother and the other could be the reporter."

Vanessa sat up in her chair. I knew I'd caught her attention.

"That's actually not a bad idea," she said, then added quickly, "but I want to be the reporter."

Of course, I thought to myself. I really didn't care. I just wanted to get through the assignment.

"No problem," I said.

We began to toss around ideas for our presentation. I did the writing. Vanessa wasn't exactly what I'd call friendly, but she didn't hiss once during the assignment. There's no audience for her to show off for, I thought. She's like a hurricane that has lost some of its bluster. One-on-one, I wasn't nearly as intimidated by her as I'd thought I'd be.

At one point I commented, "The mother in the story might have had strong reasons for what she did, but she's still a piece of work."

"She'd get along great with my mother," Vanessa said, with a snort.

I thought about the scene that I'd secretly witnessed in the parking lot between Vanessa and her mother. This English assignment was all about looking at a situation from someone else's point of view. Maybe even Vanessa's, I thought. Or her mother's. Or anyone's, for that matter.

We finished writing an outline of our presentation with five minutes to spare. Vanessa gathered up her books. I started to turn back around to my desk, but there was still the matter of the hiss. I thought about what Ben had told the group last night.

"Dare to go where you haven't gone before," he had said.

I turned back to Vanessa and looked her up and down.

"You know," I said in a serious voice, "my pink snakeskin purse would go really well with that shirt you're wearing."

Vanessa narrowed her eyes and just looked at me. I decided to take a chance and go a step further.

"I don't know why you don't like my purse," I continued with a slight grin. "A poor little hot pink snake gave its life for it, you know."

Vanessa continued to stare at me. After a few seconds I saw the flicker of a smile on her face.

"Well, I hate to tell you this," she said, "but that poor little snake died in vain."

I laughed.

"You should have seen the matching shoes," I told her.

Vanessa shook her head and rolled her eyes.

"You're something else, Marino," she said.

I was surprised that Vanessa knew my last name. Just then the bell rang.

"Presentations tomorrow," Mr. Tate called as we gathered up our things.

18: Center Stage

I'm sitting in the projection booth for the last time this semester. On the way to school tonight Mom mentioned that this is her final class of the fall session. It never occurred to me that her classes would end before Ben's.

I think back to the first night of class. So much has happened because of it. For one thing, I have Dee and Mr. Wardinski as new friends. For another thing, my thirty-second-delay switch seems to be in the "off" position lately. I've been doing pretty well at thinking on my feet. If Mr. Tate calls on me, I don't automatically panic and fumble around for words as much.

Vanessa and I acted out our interview in English class that next day. Mr. Tate gave us an A+, and the class seemed to like it, too. Vanessa actually says hi to me when she sees me in the hallway now. I doubt if we'll ever be good friends, but stranger things have happened.

And the hissing seems to be hiss-tory.

Today after class, Mr. Tate called me over to his desk.

"I love your Alexander B. Canfield character sketch," he said, handing the paper back to me. "It's very clever and well written."

Mr. Tate paused, and then he said, "Lizzie, I'm the advisor for the *Voice*."

The *Voice* is the student newspaper. Mr. Tate continued. "I was wondering if you would be interested in joining our staff. We're always looking for good writers. We meet twice a week after school."

Good writers? I thought. Me?

"Definitely," I replied.

"Great," said Mr. Tate. "Then I'll see you Monday after school right here in this room."

The most important thing that has come out of this class is my relationship with Mom. She has opened up a lot more about Dad since our little parking lot chat. One night last week she even dug out some old photo albums. We spent the evening looking through them.

One of the photos showed Dad holding Ringo

as a little puppy. Mom told me that when Ringo died, she felt like she lost one of her last connections to Dad.

"You still have me," I reminded her.

"Yes, I do," Mom agreed, hugging me.

She told me that for a long time she was afraid to let me out of her sight.

"I was afraid of losing you, too," she explained. "I guess I've been a bit overprotective at times."

"You? Overprotective? " I teased.

We laughed.

When I came home from school the next day, there was a framed wedding picture of Mom and Dad sitting on my dresser. It had been buried away in a box ever since Dad died.

Ben was right when he said that in order to succeed you have to be willing to take risks. I'm his star pupil, and he doesn't even know it.

The lights below go on. Ben walks to center stage carrying a fishing pole and a plastic garbage can. I'm perched up in my tree, ready to watch and learn.

JAN SIEBOLD is the author of the novels *Doing Time Online* and *Rope Burn*. She lives in East Aurora, New York, where she works as a school librarian.